For all the kids out there who don't want to go to sleep. I get it.
—D.P.

To my beautiful Natalie, who loves sleeping so much,
she'd probably choose to hibernate if she could.
—M.B.

Text copyright © 2018 by Dev Petty
Jacket art and interior illustrations copyright © 2018 by Mike Boldt

All rights reserved. Published in the United States by Doubleday, an imprint of Random House Children's Books,
a division of Penguin Random House LLC, New York.

Doubleday and the colophon are registered trademarks of Penguin Random House LLC.

Visit us on the Web! rhcbooks.com

Educators and librarians, for a variety of teaching tools, visit us at RHTeachersLibrarians.com

Library of Congress Cataloging-in-Publication Data
Names: Petty, Dev, author. | Boldt, Mike, illustrator.
Title: I don't want to go to sleep / by Dev Petty ; illustrated by Mike Boldt.
Description: First edition. | New York : Doubleday, [2018] | Summary: "Frog is excited about the coming of winter,
until he finds out that frogs sleep through the long cold months while they hibernate"—Provided by publisher.
Identifiers: LCCN 2017039676 (print) | LCCN 2017053136 (ebook)
ISBN 978-1-5247-6896-6 (hc) | ISBN 978-1-5247-6897-3 (glb) | ISBN 978-1-5247-6898-0 (ebook)
Subjects: | CYAC: Hibernation—Fiction. | Winter—Fiction. | Frogs—Fiction. | Humorous stories.
Classification: LCC PZ7.P448138 (ebook) | LCC PZ7.P448138 Ian 2018 (print) | DDC [E]—dc23

MANUFACTURED IN CHINA
10 9 8 7 6 5 4 3 2 1
First Edition

I DON'T WANT TO GO TO SLEEP

written by
Dev Petty

illustrated by
Mike Boldt

DOUBLEDAY BOOKS FOR YOUNG READERS

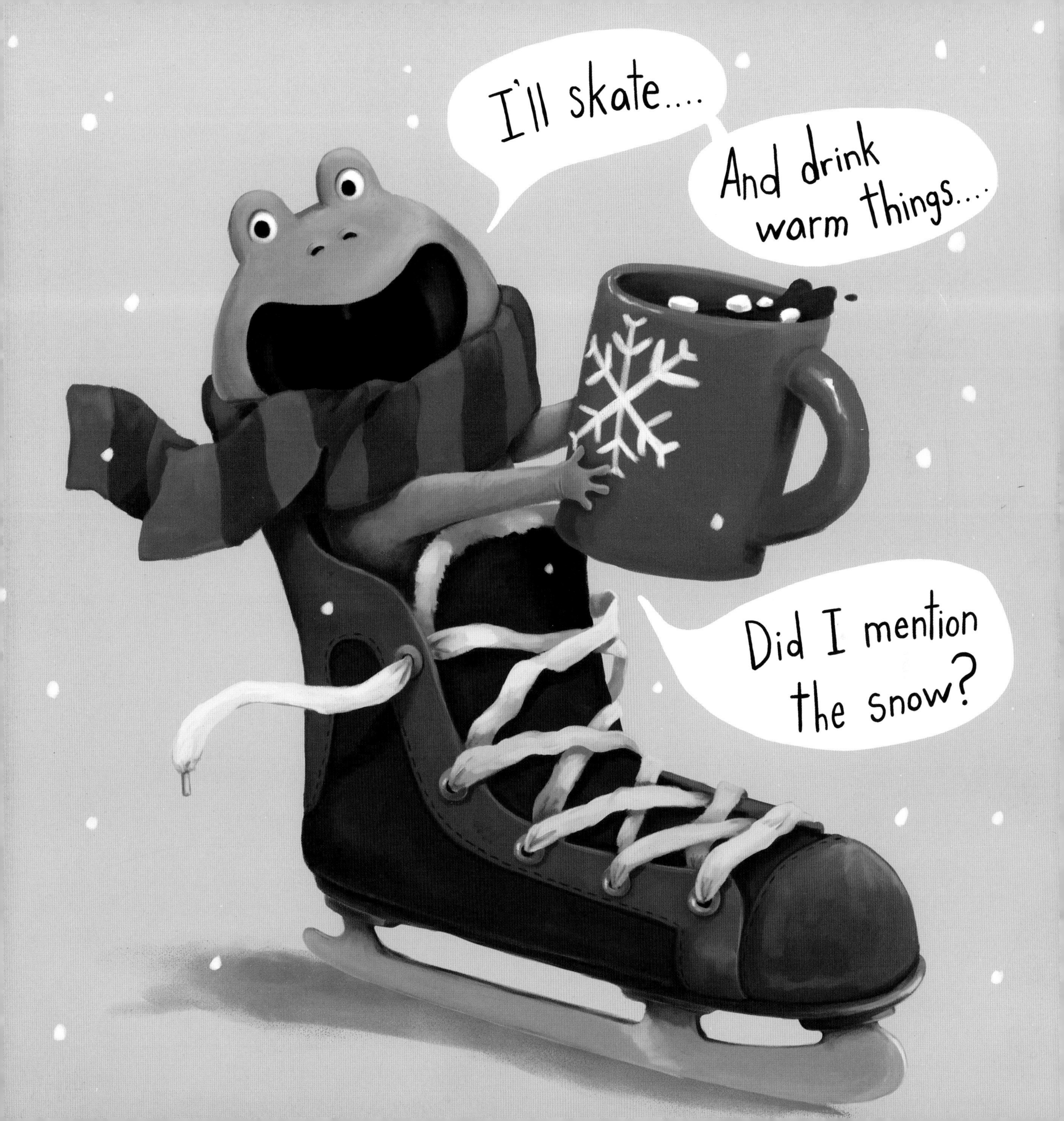
I'll skate....
And drink warm things....
Did I mention the snow?

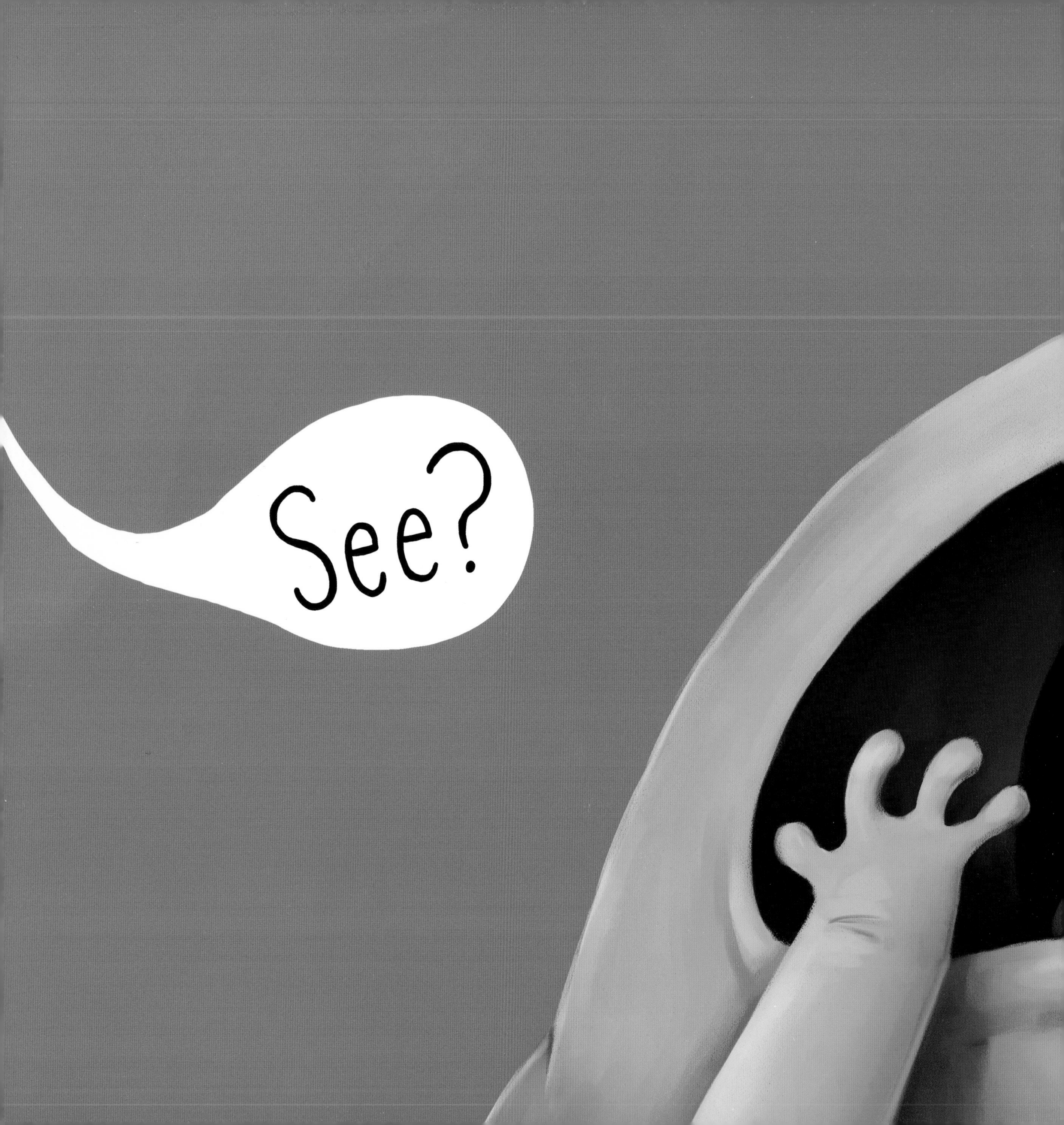
See?